Philip Waechter • Moni Port

Translated by Sally-Ann Spencer

BRAVO!

GECKO PRESS

Once upon a time, a little girl named Helena
lived in a crooked house, deep in a valley,
beside a turquoise stream.

Things were almost perfect. Helena was talented, her little brother was patient and her mother was very encouraging. Only one thing spoiled it.

Helena's father couldn't speak normally.
Everything he said came out in a roar.

WHERE ARE MY
GUMBOOTS?

I'M THIRSTY!

WHO LEFT THESE SHOES ON THE FLOOR?

MY EGG IS TOO RUNNY!

Helena didn't like it.

"What's troubling you?" her mother asked one night.

"It's Papa," whispered Helena. "He's always so noisy."

"Yes," said her mother. "He's a shouter. Shouters always shout."

"A shouter?"

"That's right."

"What makes someone a shouter?" Helena asked.

That wasn't a simple question. Helena's mother thought for a moment.
"Well," she said, "his mother was a shouter, his father was a shouter,
and his grandfather was a world-famous shouter. It runs in the family.
They've been shouters for generations. When you're older, you can
be one too, if you like."

She stroked Helena's head.

That night, Helena didn't sleep a wink.

The next morning was like every other morning.

THIS COFFE
TOO H

WHO ATE ALL
THE ORANGES?

WHO LEFT THEIR
SOCKS IN THE HALL?

Before bed, Helena stood at the window
and talked to her friend.

She lay awake, thinking.

By the morning she had reached a decision.
She packed a little suitcase with her most needed things . . .

. . . and she left the house with a spring in her step.
"Thanks for everything," she said, "but I'm not going to be a shouter."
Her brother said nothing, her mother raised her eyebrows and
her father shouted, "YOU'RE NOT GOING ANYWHERE,
DO YOU HEAR?"
Helena waved goodbye and started off up the hill.

At the top of the hill she came to a
pretty little house. Helena plucked up
her courage and knocked at the door.
A woman opened it.
"Hello, I'm Helena. May I come and
live with you?"

"But what about your mother and father?" asked the woman.

"My father's a shouter," said Helena.

"I see," said the woman and she invited Helena inside.

Helena's parents searched upstream and down.
They couldn't find her anywhere. "I miss Helena,"
her father said softly. "I'll never, ever shout again,
if only she'll come home."

Days and weeks went by, until one afternoon Helena's father saw a poster on a tree. It showed a picture of his daughter. "CONCERT" it said in big letters. And then, "Sunday at three o'clock in the town hall."

The family was overjoyed. They could hardly wait. They were going to see Helena again!

The big day arrived.

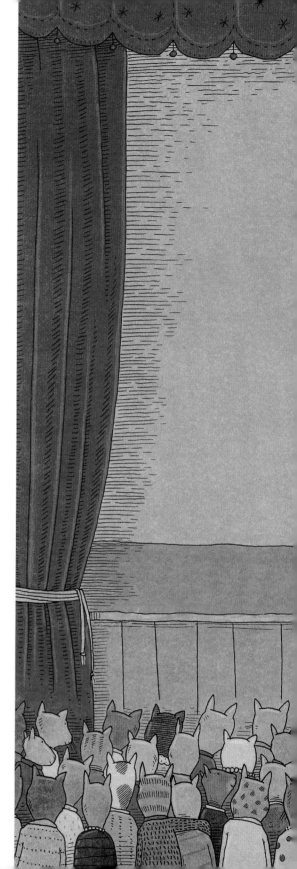

The concert was amazing.
Fabulous. Fantastic.
Too good for words.
Everyone was quiet as a mouse.

The curtain fell to thunderous applause.
The audience clapped and clapped.
Only one person shouted.

BRAVO!

But this time, Helena was
happy to hear him.